HEROI
LAST NIGHT

A PLAY IN TWO ACTS

by Ian Smith

HEROD'S LAST NIGHT
Copyright © 2010 by Ian Smith

ISBN 978 – 1 – 4467 – 1388 - 4

Introduction.

What follows is a dark comedy in the 'I, Claudius' style that follows the fictitious final hours of one of the ancient world's best-known and most notorious figures: Herod the Great, who for decades managed the Roman province of Judaea on behalf of Octavian Augustus, first of the emperors. Herod was, in many ways, the Stalin of first-century Asia: ruthless, ambitious, cruel, wearing self-preservation like armour. When he believed himself threatened, no-one was safe: his officials, wives and even sons met their ends at an alarming rate; and yet he was in other ways a fine ruler. Steeped in Hellenistic culture, he embellished his country with splendid buildings; in time of famine, he sold personal valuables to buy the people bread; he subdued banditry, stabilised and developed the nation and above all kept the emperor happy and the Roman war machine at bay. His career was colourful, dramatic: a young leader given power by the Roman invaders, he became involved with the fabled Anthony and Cleopatra during Rome's internal power struggles; he embarked on a fairytale romance with the beautiful Jewish princess Mariamne; he provided the Jewish people with the most beautiful building in Asia: Jerusalem's Second Temple, where Jesus worshipped and whose destruction he foresaw.

Alas, this remarkable King of the Jews was never really accepted by his Jewish subjects. To begin with, he wasn't Jewish, but of Idumean stock; he ruled on behalf of the detested gentile overlords in Italy; and he seemed to benefit and provoke his subjects in equal measure. No doubt this contributed to his growing paranoia as his health failed towards the end of his life.

Then there was the 'Bethlehem Incident', better known as the Massacre of the Innocents, for which Herod has been remembered with horror every Christmas. Hearing that a child of a rival royal line had apparently been born in Bethlehem (at a time when a *real* Jewish king like the Maccabean freedom fighters of old was very much wanted), Herod resolved the situation and protected his dynasty by ordering the murder of all Bethlehemite boys who were old enough to fit the bill. The truth of this has been questioned on the grounds that there is no known record of the incident outside the Gospels, whose account naturally emphasises the infant Jesus' narrow escape.

Although one can see the point of this argument, I think the absence of other records of the atrocity is unsurprising. When one considers the very high mortality rate of people in close (or not so close) proximity to Herod, including his immediate family, along with his severe paranoia and the widespread resentment of Rome and her client kings, implementing a relatively small number of deaths (by Herodian standards) in an obscure peasant community isn't difficult to imagine; and why record the passing of these very minor casualties of history? True, Herod is mentioned only briefly in the Gospels because of his connection with Jesus' early life, but the larger picture of this dangerous man shows the Bethlehem assassinations to be very much in character; and since it was all done in the interests of the State, perhaps he just forgot about it. If he was able to, that is…

CHARACTERS:

TIMON ATHENAGORAS, Personal servant to Herod.

ZIBEAH, an aristocratic Jewish lady

NABAL, a general in Herod's army

HEROD, King of Judea

THE HIGH PRIEST

A PRISON GUARD

A MESSENGER

GUARDS

All Herod's 'back story' referred to by himself and others (his career, family, the Temple, relations with his subjects) is true. Any good history books or Who's Who of the ancient world will fill in the details of the times and the individuals.

The good history books will not tell you the stories of Timon, Zibeah and the other characters of the play as they and their involvement with Herod are purely fictitious. Likewise, the circumstances of Herod's death were not as depicted here.

Think of it all as a jewel of fiction in a setting of fact and enjoy it.

HEROD'S LAST NIGHT

Act One: The Lady At The Banquet.

(Spotlight on TIMON, seated downstage to one side.)

TIMON: I lean back into my seat under the vines by the little statue in the garden of my villa and look out over my estate. The evening breeze comes up from the sea and I watch the sunlight falling over my fields and on the white temples of Athens; and I think, here I am – Timon Athenagoras, the most unlikely landowner in the empire.

Why am I here? The reason spans almost my whole life, yet I only learned it in the few moments that summed up all my years in the court of Herod the Great.

Imagine the evening of the annual banquet. The palace at Jerusalem is filled with the mighty ones of the empire – Jews, Romans, Greeks, Persians, all in awe of Herod; but now that he's old and sick they think it's safe to despise him and call him mad. Behind his back of course; they haven't the courage to come out and say it. And I am upstairs in a little private room with a couch and a table. This is where Herod will be, and this is where I bring the supper tray.

(Lights up on the set, a sumptuous private room in Herod's palace. Downstage centre is a large couch laden with cushions and with small tables beside it where wine and sweetmeats are set out. To one side is a conspicuous table with an assortment of jars and medicine bottles. Farther to the side is a Roman-style female statue. TIMON takes up the supper tray and begins to busy himself about the room.)

Now then, let's get your supper set out, your majesty: spiced chicken and larks' tongues in aspic, guaranteed not poisoned. Or if they are you'll soon be looking for a new personal servant. And here's your wine, Tuscan vineyards of course and just enough to get you to sleep but keep you sober. Reasonably sober. I do think you made the right decision about the banquet: you're really *not* well enough, your majesty, and they can get on perfectly well without you, as you well know. They only come to stuff their faces and get looked at: they couldn't care less about *you*, King of the

Jews. *(Pause)* They're all here: High Priest, Chief Scribe, Roman ambassador and that great fat eunuch from Persia that comes every year: all the usual crawlers, cashing in their free meal ticket from the greatest king in Asia, Herod the Great. You leave them to it, I say. There's only one person in this palace cares about you, I hope you realise, just one. Just one. *(Abruptly changes his own subject)* You have a quiet night in with your feet up. Speaking of which, do we have the ointment? Yes we do. And we have the bandages and the dressings and the Pongy Salve. On the medicine front...one, two, three...yes, all there, and on the Dire Emergency front we have the Red Bottle and, heaven forbid, the Green Bottle. But let's not talk about that. I've got to get you here for supper, so please, please, don't go dotty and wander off, not tonight. Please, not tonight.

(He leaves. ZIBEAH enters.)

ZIBEAH: Hello? Hello? Anyone at home? Thank goodness, peace at last. Oh, and some rather nice delicacies. Mm, spiced chicken. Better than they've got downstairs.

(Enter NABAL.)

NABAL: Zibeah! I thought it was you. What are you doing here? These are private rooms.

ZIBEAH: Well, General Nabal. You're looking *so* sweet in your dress uniform. As for what I'm doing here, isn't it obvious? I'm attending King Herod's banquet.

NABAL: What? With Uzzah so ill? He's your husband! Why aren't you with him?

ZIBEAH: Well it's a nice change from bedpans and stinking poultices, but mainly I'm representing the family. It's in our interests. You should understand that, Nabal.

NABAL: Uzzah should be representing the family. I'd have stopped you if I'd known.

ZIBEAH: Nabal, you can't. Besides, what do you want Uzzah to do? Leap out of bed and charge down here to Jerusalem? Not an option, dear. It was me or nothing.

NABAL: Are you saying he's worse?

ZIBEAH: You hadn't heard? It's really just a matter of time now, so if I were you I'd apply for compassionate leave so you can go and hold your little brother's hand for the last time.

NABAL: I wish I'd seen through you before father arranged the marriage. It would never have happened.

ZIBEAH: Well, in a way I sympathise with that. I've had twelve of the most boring years imaginable. I won't hide it from you, Nabal: I'll be glad to breathe the free air again. It isn't just the money, although there'll be lots of that. It's – oh, what could I say? – the opportunity.

NABAL: Opportunity?

ZIBEAH: Of course. It was a good family to marry into, I've scored a lot of points. But now – what next? I'll be free enough and just young enough to make an even better match. And who knows what next? Frankly, dear, Uzzah was just a rung on the ladder.

NABAL: Why did you marry him, Zibeah? Why did you inflict yourself on our family?

ZIBEAH: I told you, dear: opportunity. And don't think I haven't paid a price: I've tolerated Uzzah's deadly tedium too long – I deserve the release. Oh, don't worry: I'll do some decent mourning. But if I'd known he was going to be a provincial financial official I might have thought twice: he's a human abacus.

NABAL: Don't provoke me, Zibeah. Why didn't you stay at the banquet?

ZIBEAH: Fresh air, dear. The Romans are being obnoxious. Do you know what that cow Jocasta said to me?

NABAL: No, but you deserved it. Now come away before you're arrested.

ZIBEAH: Oh, I think I'll stay. I might meet Herod.

NABAL: Don't be ridiculous.

ZIBEAH: He must be up here somewhere. If he's not at the banquet, where is he?

NABAL: In bed. He has a fever.

ZIBEAH: Oh, you're so *loyal!* Admit it: he's having a mad turn: he's roaming the corridors calling for his murdered wife.

NABAL: Have some respect.

ZIBEAH: Well, why do you think he's lasted so long? He's assassinated everybody who as much as looked at the throne. Or criticised him, or was too popular, or too good-looking.

NABAL: He has the confidence of the Emperor.

ZIBEAH: Just as well. The people can't stand him: King of the Jews and he's not even Jewish.

NABAL: He's made this province a greatly admired nation.

ZIBEAH: Before he was mad. But I suppose he does well for us – those of us that behave, anyway. Actually, you know, I took my life in my hands coming down here to the palace. You don't know who the old maniac's going to go for next. You know what they say: 'Safer to be Herod's pig than Herod's son.' And speaking of sons, where's Prince Antipater? He's not at the banquet.

NABAL: His Highness is – detained.

ZIBEAH: Detained? Oh, the dungeon! How juicy! What charge?

NABAL: Suspicion of conspiring to usurp the throne. Only suspicion, mind.

ZIBEAH: Well, he's either innocent or stupid. He ought to know Herod hasn't got long left.

NABAL: Yes, but Antipater isn't in the running.

ZIBEAH: Oh. Herod's imagined it, then?

NABAL: They're gathering evidence.

ZIBEAH: How? Thumbscrews? There won't be anyone left to succeed him at this rate.

NABAL: That's tasteless, Zibeah.

ZIBEAH: Not as tasteless as murdering three of your sons. And your wife. And your wife's mother.

NABAL: They were legally executed.

ZIBEAH: Oh, well, that's all right then. Unlike his brother-in-law.

NABAL: Ah yes. The swimming accident.

ZIBEAH: That's the one: when those silly men inadvertently held him under the water. For ten minutes. So careless. And the sad case of the High Council. Imagine – forty-six dear old clergymen having a collective coronary. Probably the shock of seeing those nasty men with swords. And was it one High Priest or two - ?

NABAL: That was over thirty years ago. The authority structure has stabilised.

ZIBEAH: Ah yes. Where would society be without those nice keen boys of the liquidation squad? They say they're so hunky in that shiny armour.

NABAL: Zibeah, I'd almost say you enjoyed all this.

ZIBEAH: Well it is sort of morbidly fascinating. Anyway, everyone likes a good story and it's so tedious up there in Trachonitis. Court gossip makes the time pass wonderfully. Come to think of it, Nabal, you've lasted quite a while yourself. Cushy number, of course: military Chief of Staff –

NABAL: I make my contribution. I shall continue to serve.

ZIBEAH: An example to us all. Mind you...

NABAL: What?

ZIBEAH: Quite a catch.

NABAL: A catch? Who are you - ? Oh. You can't be serious! Zibeah! How could you - ?

ZIBEAH: My little joke, Nabal. Why should I set myself up as a target? Besides, who'd marry that geriatric bag of ailments? What do you suppose I could be thinking of?

NABAL: You could be thinking of Uzzah. Good night, Zibeah

ZIBEAH: Well, it might not be so bad. *(TIMON enters)* Hail, Queen Zibeah. Zibeah, Queen of the Jews.

TIMON: Can I help you?

ZIBEAH: I don't think so.

TIMON: These are *private* apartments, madam.

ZIBEAH: And you are?

TIMON: My name is Timon Athenagoras and I'm personal servant to King Herod.

ZIBEAH: Oh. Well, now we've been introduced, buzz off. On second thoughts, bring me some wine.

TIMON: I'm personal servant to *King Herod*, madam. Now I must ask you to return to the banquet.

ZIBEAH: Fiercely loyal, I see.

TIMON: Yes, I am.   But if necessary, a more senior person can be brought.   Now I

really must ask -

(A GUARD enters)

GUARD: Timon, you'd better come quick!   He got away from the nurses - he's pretty bad.

TIMON: Where is he?

GUARD: Dunno, we've lost him.

TIMON: Lost him?   How could you have lost him?   *(To Zibeah:)* Madam, excuse me.

(TIMON exits with the SERVANT.)

ZIBEAH: You just can't get decent staff nowadays.   When I am queen, vile minions, I shall surround myself with more worthy servants.

(HEROD enters.)

Oh.   You must be the more senior person.   Well, I can tell you I've no intention of moving, so you can totter off and find someone even more senior than yourself.   If that's possible.   And when you find them tell them to bring me wine.

HEROD: Have you seen my wife?   I was looking for my wife.   I sent her away, you see; she must be very upset by now.

ZIBEAH: I haven't seen your wife.   Perhaps she's at the banquet.

HEROD: I've been looking for her for ages, ever since I sent her away. She must be terribly upset.   Oh, is that supper?

(HEROD begins to sample the dishes set out.)

ZIBEAH: I really don't think you should do that.

HEROD: Oh, it's all right, it's for me and my wife, you see. We like to sit here and have a little supper together. I can't think where she's got to. You haven't seen her, have you? You haven't seen my wife?

ZIBEAH: No, I haven't. She ought to be in bed by now, a woman of her age.

HEROD: Oh, she's not in bed. I'd know if she was. She has such cold feet. That's a very pretty dress.

ZIBEAH: It's a Roman style. Pinches a little under the arms. But I must say I'm regretting this Roman hairstyle – far too severe. I really prefer my hair down: I need to relax.

HEROD: I'm going to miss the banquet. I'm a little off-colour tonight.

ZIBEAH: If I just take these combs out… There, that's better.

HEROD: And my wife won't be there: too many people she doesn't like: those Roman matrons can be quite obnoxious. I'm surprised you haven't seen her. Everybody in the palace knows her: a charming woman, a lovely, charming woman - *(He turns and sees Zibeah with her hair down.)* Oh! Oh, my darling, there you are! With your beautiful air around your shoulders. Oh, don't leave me again! I'll never send you away again, I promise you. Do stay, I've been so terribly lonely -

(TIMON dashes in, hearing the noise. He is greatly relieved to find Herod.)

TIMON: What's going on? Oh, *there* you are. Did we give our nurses the slip, then? Cunning old majesty.

ZIBEAH: This is nothing to do with me. He just started wailing –

HEROD: I've found her, Timon. I've found the queen. My dear Mariamne: she's come back to me. You look just as you did on the quay at Caesarea when I jumped from the boat before they even had the gangplank out, I was so eager to be with you. Do you remember? The breeze in your lovely hair and the sunlight vying with your shining eyes. Your dress of silk and gold, the flowers you'd woven around your head. We must have a little party. Timon, you go to the kitchen -

TIMON: No, no, no. Look closely: that's not the queen.

HEROD: Of course it's the queen. Look at her: look at her wonderful hair –

TIMON: Ah, but Mariamne's hair's all thick and frizzy, isn't it? And she always has different ornaments in it.

HEROD: Well, who's that, then?

TIMON: This is a lady who's come for the banquet. Lady, er –

ZIBEAH: Zibeah. Of the house of ben Sirach. *(Curtseys)*

HEROD: Well, where's the queen? Isn't she in her suite?

TIMON: The queen lives in Egypt now, remember? You sent her to Egypt to live with Cleopatra.

HEROD: Did I? Yes, of course. *(To Zibeah:)* Not that I'm sure that was a wise move. Cleopatra was wildly in love with me, you see. I invited her to our wedding, but of course she didn't come. Not even a present. I hope my wife's enjoying herself down there.

TIMON: Oh yes, they'll have lots to talk about. Now let's get along, shall we? I've got your water closet ready.

HEROD: Is it that time already? Ah well. Good night, my dear, very nice to have met you. You have such lovely hair.

TIMON: Well, off we go then.

HEROD: Yes, yes, I'll manage. Good night, good night...

ZIBEAH: Was that him? Was that really Herod? He was so *nice!*

TIMON: Yes, it was, and I would beg discretion on your part. Stories circulate, you know –

ZIBEAH: What was all that about my hair?

TIMON: His majesty was a little confused. The late queen had long dark hair not unlike your own.

ZIBEAH: He thought I was Mariamne! He was actually in love with me!

TIMON: Only for fifteen seconds. Don't get your hopes up.

ZIBEAH: Is he always like that? Mad all the time?

TIMON: Certainly not. His majesty can be very…alert. Very normal.

ZIBEAH: Or something in between. I know what you're not saying. I expect all the murders drove him over the edge. Especially Mariamne.

TIMON: Those are wicked lies.

ZIBEAH: That's very loyal of you, dear, but everybody knows. Just accept it.

TIMON: Well, as I said before, these are private apartments, so, er….

ZIBEAH: Of course. I'll find my own way out. You see to his majesty.

TIMON: Yes, I think I'd better. I'll bid you goodnight, then.

ZIBEAH: Very nice to meet you, Timon. I'm sorry I was a little sharp.

TIMON: That's all right. Now, I've got to go, excuse me.

ZIBEAH: Fifteen seconds. Not bad for the first meeting. Well, off I go. Oh; such a warm night. I probably won't need this scarf. I may as well just drape it here. Tastefully, on this couch. By accident.

TIMON: Thank you, your majesty, for agreeing to the bath. Your body-slaves'll have you all pink and glowing and scrubbed to perfection. And sleepy. I hope. Because I wouldn't mind just nodding off myself. That is a *very* fetching scarf. *Beautiful* fabric: very finely woven, and so delicate. Hardly any weight at all around the shoulders. Really clever colour: unusual, eye-catching, but not ostentatious. It's just not the sort of thing Herod would wear.

(NABAL enters.)

Oh, general Nabal! What can I do for you?

NABAL: Sit down, Timon, you need a rest.

TIMON: Oh, I do. I've just got him to go for a bath. Told the slaves to take their time. You're not enjoying the banquet, then?

NABAL: Oh, it's the usual babble. I'm rather running out of small talk. Besides, I'm a little preoccupied.

TIMON: Will you have a jar with me, then? It's not what they're serving downstairs, you know. This is from the private cellar, if you get my meaning.

NABAL: Oh. Well, perhaps just a mouthful.

TIMON: Yes, go on, he'll never know. *(Pours.)*

NABAL: I say, that's very fine stuff. It's practically dishwater downstairs by comparison.

TIMON: Did you want him? He won't be about tonight.

NABAL: No, I was actually looking for someone. She should be downstairs, but I last saw her here. Tall woman, dark hair, Roman-style dress - . You're wearing her scarf, Timon. The scarf. Round your shoulder. You've seen her?

TIMON: Couldn't get rid of her. She was sitting here as if she owned the place. Had quite a long conversation with himself. He thought she was Mariamne. I think she quite liked the idea. *(Mimics Zibeah.)* 'He was in love with me.'

NABAL: In love with her? *(Horrible thought.)* Oh no. Oh, surely not.

TIMON: Something wrong?

NABAL: No, no. I need to…give her a message.

TIMON: Friend of yours?

NABAL: My sister-in-law, as a matter of fact. Her husband's ill – my brother – and we need to, er, discuss it. You know, family talk.

TIMON: Oh, I'm sorry, general. If I can do anything -

NABAL: Thank you, Timon, you gave me your sympathy. And good wine.

(ZIBEAH enters.)

ZIBEAH: Oh, *do* excuse me. Is this a private party?

TIMON: The party's downstairs, madam.

NABAL: Zibeah, you have no legitimate reason to be in these apartments.

ZIBEAH: Whereas you can just walk in. Give me some of that wine.

NABAL: I'm in charge of his majesty's military affairs. I have permanent access.

ZIBEAH: Of course. Well, my excuse isn't nearly so good. Silly little me forgot my scarf. It came all the way from Memphis, terribly expensive, so I couldn't possibly just leave it here, now could I?

NABAL: Well, you've got it. Now go back to the banquet.

ZIBEAH: So soon? I thought I might give my regards to the dear old king.

NABAL: Zibeah, the truth. Are you even remotely serious about trying to marry Herod?

ZIBEAH: Nabal! Don't be so rough!

NABAL: Tell me!

ZIBEAH: I don't like frontal attacks. You're not on campaign.

NABAL: But I think you are. He thought you were Mariamne, you thought he was in love with you. Yes, I know. He's a mad old man, Zibeah, leave him alone. Haven't you used all your cruelty on our family?

ZIBEAH: You seem to think I owe you something, Nabal. I don't know what debt you're trying to collect, but I'd be deeply grateful if you didn't get in my way. *(Herod enters)*

HEROD: Timon? Timon, I can't sleep.

ZIBEAH *(To Nabal)* : I think you understand me, Nabal.

HEROD: And who have we here? Don't tell me, don't tell me – the Egyptian ambassador.

TIMON: Why not have a drink with the ambassador? A little sip of this, eh? *(Whisper)* It's his medicine. There we are.

HEROD: Oh, very poor wine! I do apologise, your Excellency. Now, if it's about the grain subsidy –

TIMON: And just look who's come to say hello. *(Herod's head clears.)*

HEROD: General Nabal, how nice. And I think I know *you* –

ZIBEAH: The lady Zibeah, of the house of ben Sirach. Your majesty honoured me with your conversation earlier. *(Laughs)* I left my scarf. How silly. Um…your majesty was kind enough to complement me on my hair. I'm wearing it down tonight. For a change.

TIMON: Madam Zibeah, I think we -

HEROD: Your hair. Yes, I believe I did. Very fine hair, very…haunting.

ZIBEAH: Your majesty's company was so…warming. I'll…always remember.

HEROD: Then why not have some more of it? Timon, some wine for the lady. You'll join us, general?

NABAL: Sire, forgive me. I'm required downstairs.

HEROD: Let me select some sweetmeats for you, my dear.

(TIMON busies himself with the dishes. As he does so, ZIBEAH pulls him over and hisses in his ear.)

ZIBEAH: Timon, come here. Is he mad?

TIMON: What?

ZIBEAH: Mad or sane? Does he know what he's saying?

TIMON: Well, sane, actually.

ZIBEAH: Perfectly normal?

TIMON: Yes!

ZIBEAH: Right.

HEROD: Well, well, Zibeah of ben Sirach. Don't look surprised. I've seen you at every palace reception since you were married. I see, I hear and I remember. I'm completely informed about everyone of the slightest significance in this kingdom. Including the vigorous, ambitious and spirited wife of Uzzah ben Sirach. And by the way, my congratulations on your spouse's rapid and most promising deterioration.

TIMON: Sire! You can't say that!

HEROD: Timon, I am the king, like this lady I am a realist, and I'm generally acknowledged to be more than a little ga-ga. I think I can say what I like. Besides, madam, I don't think I'm giving anything away if I say your husband is the most uninteresting man I've ever met. A superb grasp of financial administration, but deadly boring. I don't know how you've stood the tedium all these years. You must have been demented.

ZIBEAH: Your majesty has great insight.

HEROD: Oh, a remark here, an observation there, a conversation reported: everything reaches me. I know all about your frustration. A woman of your calibre should have made a better match. Something more stimulating.

ZIBEAH: Uzzah has been a good husband to me. Within his limitations.

HEROD: And he's growing more limited every day from what I hear. Who do you have in mind?

ZIBEAH: Sire?

HEROD: Oh, come, come. A woman like you must be looking ahead. You won't be moping around in widow's weeds for the rest of your life, you're not the type.

ZIBEAH: Well, sire, it's true that, alas, I will soon be alone. But who will protect me and provide for me then I do not know.

HEROD: I expect Uzzah's money will provide for you. As for protection, I think you'd see to that yourself very well.

ZIBEAH: One gathers one's resources as best one can. But what a fine and generous judge of character you are, sire. And how understanding. You, of course, will know the longing that the absence of a companion can bring. How tragic that you must rule alone. *(Gasps, as if she has shocked herself.)* Forgive me, I have spoken quite out of turn! It was just that, for a wonderful moment, I felt such…compassion.

HEROD: I'm deeply moved. So, you think I should marry?

ZIBEAH: Oh, far be it from me –

HEROD: No, no, don't be shy. Any suggestions?

ZIBEAH: Well, if I may presume… Your majesty would need to marry someone of an old and aristocratic Jewish family, with connections to a royal line if possible. To ensure acceptance by the people, you see, and to strengthen your position.

HEROD: Good point. Carry on.

ZIBEAH: She should have some knowledge of provincial administration and court life and be – what can I say? – a spirited person, a woman of inner strength, determination, who could help you rule. And of course – may I say it? – *(seductive)* one who could be your...companion, the comfort of your intimate hours, one who could...cherish you.

HEROD: You've certainly given it some thought. And how amazing!

ZIBEAH: Amazing, sire?

HEROD: Yes, the most astonishing coincidence. If I'm not mistaken, it describes you exactly. I can't vouch for the cherishing bit, of course, but all the rest – it's you to a T!

ZIBEAH: Gosh! Why – yes! Isn't it amazing what one says without realising? Goodness, your majesty is so perceptive. Mind you – I'd certainly do the cherishing! Oh! There I go! Do excuse me!

HEROD: Not at all, not at all. Timon, will you bring me the bundle wrapped in the yellow cloth?

TIMON: Er – are you sure?

HEROD: Quite sure.

TIMON: You don't think it's a bit too - ?

HEROD: Bring me the bundle, Timon. *(To Zibeah)* You see, my dear, any wife of mine would have a very busy life. She'd certainly have to be on her toes. Ah, the bundle. Thank you, Timon. I thought I'd show you this beautiful dagger, my dear. A symbol of my wealth and power, so to speak. You see the alabaster handle, the blade superbly inlaid with ivory and silver. Where was I? Yes, it's not all feasting and lounging around here, you know, got a kingdom to run. You never know what's coming next.

ZIBEAH: Oh! Your majesty! You're hurting me!

HEROD: So you want to marry Herod! Then feel this dagger at your throat and see the true Herod before you.. No madman now, no amiable dodderer to cajole. I have returned, I am The Great, the scourge in the hand of Rome, the professional tyrant. I am the lion, ravenous; I am the insatiable desert, the furnace, the scorpion. Will you dare my sting? Will you be one flesh with the royal beast of Asia? You think I'm a complete fool? You think I can't see through you and your performance? Are you strong enough? Are you my match? Are you up to the job, Queen of the Jews? I wonder. Well? Give me an answer.

ZIBEAH *(Terrified):* Your majesty – your majesty is – wise.

HEROD: Wise? What d'you mean, wise?

ZIBEAH: However - tactful I tried to be, there had to be – a test. I knew that. One cannot settle these things – lightly.

HEROD: Tactful? How tactful?

ZIBEAH: To avoid offence. To show – respect.

HEROD: Respect. *(He lowers the dagger.)* That's a good answer, Zibeah of ben Sirach. There; sit up. You're a quick thinker under pressure, I like that. Many have thought too slowly for me. *(He rises.)* Well, make yourself at home. Not that I'm promising anything.

TIMON *('Naughty-naughty' tone)*: Sire, excuse me. Where are you off to?

HEROD: Timon, I am an elderly gentleman who's drunk a great deal of watered-down wine. Where do you think I'm off to?

(HEROD exits. ZIBEAH collapses, gasping.)

ZIBEAH: I thought you said he was sane!

TIMON: He is. Perfectly sane. Which, to some people, is the problem. I'll just put this little trinket away.

ZIBEAH: He's acting like a maniac! You call that sane?

TIMON: Yes, I do. He knows exactly what he's doing. You've just had the dagger test. They all did, all his wives. And all the hopefuls. You said it yourself: you can't settle these things lightly. But don't worry, dear, you did very well. I've seen mighty matriarchs yelp like dogs and run for their lives. There was a cousin of the High Priest that sat up like an empress and said, 'Run me through if you must, but I will never submit to such theatricals.' Then she was sick and fainted. She failed, of course, thank goodness. She was a mean old buzzard.

ZIBEAH: You mean it's calculated?

TIMON: Of course. It's a bit drastic, I admit, but it certainly sorts out – well, not exactly the men from the boys, but you know what I mean. You don't just sit about and crochet if you're married to Herod the Great.

ZIBEAH: Even Mariamne had the dagger test? Even her?

TIMON: Well, that was a bit before my time, but actually no, I don't think she did. She got through for other reasons.

ZIBEAH: He really loved her?

TIMON: Everybody did. She was a real fairy-tale princess, descended straight from the old Jewish kings and as lovely as the day was long. Herod was totally, madly in love with her. He was her prince charming. He cut quite a dashing figure in those days.

ZIBEAH: He cut more than that. What happened?

TIMON: Something – went wrong. He changed: I think he felt frightened and threatened. He thought people were trying to take his place and he couldn't stand it.

ZIBEAH: So heads rolled, literally. But they say a lot of it was his imagination.

TIMON: Yes, I think so, some of it. There were plots all the time, of course –

ZIBEAH: Was *she* plotting?

TIMON: He thought she was. I don't know. But he got the idea into his head and nothing could shake it.

ZIBEAH: So she had to go. The old story – love versus power.

TIMON: No, love versus fear. *(Turns to confront Zibeah.)* It's not because he's a monster. He's not well: there's something wrong with him.

ZIBEAH: Ah, the compassionately insightful interpretation. It does explain all these bottles. Well, you might be right. We used to hear about the latest assassinations up in Trachonitis. The officials used to bet on who'd be next – rather tasteless. But our monarch seems to have calmed down in recent years. There was a very vague story, just this time of year, banquet time – something happened in a little village…Bethany, or Bethlehem, one of those places, but we couldn't think who could have upset him in a place like that. You wouldn't know, would you?

TIMON: Sounds like the rumour mill to me. Will you have more wine?

ZIBEAH: It was several years ago, and we haven't heard of anything since. It seems this palace is a safer place to be. *(Timon pours wine.)* Oh: now I think of it there *was* a story a year or two later, quite amusing for a change. Apparently three Persian diplomats turned up here at the palace, complete entourage, military escort, everything, and asked to pay their respects to Herod's baby son, the new King of the Jews. Well, of course there wasn't a baby son – terrible embarrassment all round. There was an enquiry, a few heads at Diplomatic Intelligence rolled and dispatches went back and forth to Persia for months. They never found out who blundered. But you're a survivor, Timon Athenagoras. Why hasn't your head rolled?

TIMON: I'm not plotting. I don't want to be king.

ZIBEAH: But he might have imagined you do. Look, you talk to him like a five-year-old. You practically order him about. People have been hanged for less.

TIMON: His majesty needs a little direction. When he's, er…

ZIBEAH: When he's mad. Well, how did you get the job?

TIMON: Oh, it was all long ago. Doesn't matter.

ZIBEAH: Tell me, Timon. Or when I'm queen, I'll make you.

TIMON: Well. Our family was Greek, you see. I lived in Athens with my mother – my dad died when I was two - and when I was still young we sailed across here with my uncle to visit people at Caesarea, on the coast. We went for a trip inland one day and a swarm of bandits came down on us. They were going to make off with me when Herod turned up.

ZIBEAH: In shining armour? *(Timon has to bite his tongue for a moment.)*

TIMON: In a way. He was inspecting the patrols near Caesarea and his detachment ran into the bandits. Made short work of them, of course – not one left standing. But Herod went straight for the ones that had a hold of me and fought them like a fury: three of them, but they hadn't a chance. It was so brave of him. Then he kicked their heads aside and knelt down in front of me with his hands on my shoulders. 'I'm the king,' he said. 'I'll look after you.'

ZIBEAH: What did your mother say?

TIMON: Nothing: she was dead. So was my uncle. Herod saw it and said to me, 'I'm very sorry. Would you like to come and live with me now?' Well, what was I to do? I'd no other family and all I could see was this big, kind man who'd saved my life when he might have got killed himself. I suddenly felt all safe and grateful, so I just said 'Yes', then put my arms round his neck and cried and cried. And, er, that was that. Would you – would you like more wine?

ZIBEAH: So, he has his moments after all. Nice to know that a man who's executed most of his sons can come over all paternal. Yes, I will have a little more.

TIMON: Well, I'm in his debt. He saved my life and I won't hear a word said against him.

ZIBEAH: With his record, that must be difficult. *(Timon is really stung this time.)*

TIMON: Well, with some things, people's *records* just don't matter.

ZIBEAH: Ohh, the little Greek worm is turning. Don't get angry with me, dearie, I'm not a bandit.

TIMON: I'm not so sure.

ZIBEAH: What do you mean by that?

TIMON: You're as cruel and vicious as the men that killed my mother. You're no better, you're no different: you'll take what you can get, you'll hurt anybody –

ZIBEAH: Watch your mouth, you pagan.

TIMON: You like it, don't you? You like hurting and lying. You feel powerful or something. Well, I've seen it all before: the court's full of people like you: highfalutin', overdressed – bandits.

ZIBEAH: Take that back! Take it back! How dare you! Do you know who you're talking to? Do you know what I can do to you - ?

HEROD: Getting to know each other?

TIMON: All well, sire?

HEROD: All well, Timon. Zibeah, my dear, I have to conduct an important interview in a few minutes. Perhaps you wouldn't mind just powdering your nose for a little while. I'll send for you.

ZIBEAH: I will be ready for your majesty's summons.

HEROD: Come here. I thought I heard a raised voice. Who could possibly be speaking like that to Timon? I wondered. I would be very sorry if Timon were ever treated badly, now or at any time *in the future.*

ZIBEAH: I too would be sorry. I would hate anyone to upset your majesty.

HEROD: Good. Now run along.

(ZIBEAH exits.)

TIMON: Sire, about that woman –

HEROD: I know, Timon, I heard some of it. But let's talk about it later. You know it's that time of year again, banquet time –

TIMON: I was going to say. Are you managing?

HEROD: Difficult, Timon, difficult. I've sent downstairs for the High Priest, he's on his way now. The irony of it: I'm not even Jewish.

TIMON: I'm sure he'll be helpful. She was talking about it, you know.

HEROD: Was she? Why?

TIMON: Oh, just coincidence, I expect. Conversation.

HEROD: She didn't make anything of it?

TIMON: No, she'd just heard a rumour years ago. But she did try to pump me for information. Didn't give her any of course.

HEROD: Good lad, Timon. I shall need to look at lady Zibeah very closely.

TIMON: Oh, *sire* –

HEROD: Some things are worth tolerating.

(THE HIGH PRIEST enters, eating from a dish.)

Ah, our High Priest. Timon, will you excuse us?

(TIMON exits.)

Enjoying the banquet, Your Grace?

HIGH PRIEST: An extremely well-managed event, your majesty. This is a very fine example of lamb's liver.

HEROD: Everything's kosher too, I made sure. And it's all been checked for poison.

HIGH PRIEST: Your majesty is satirical.

HEROD: Far be it from me to poison the High Priest. Oh, was that a shock? I know what you're thinking: you're thinking about the Jewish High Council when I became king, now aren't you?

HIGH PRIEST: Their terminations can spring to mind.

HEROD: Ah, yes. Well, I had to, you see; you know that. I'd only just been appointed: I had to establish a dynasty, consolidate rule. How could I with those reactionary old farts breathing down my neck?

HIGH PRIEST: As always, your Majesty resolutely applied your mind to political realities.

HEROD: Well put, very well put. I have always pursued stability, unity.

HIGH PRIEST: Thoughts keenly focussed and unclouded by sentiment.

HEROD: Security of the realm. I have never shirked responsible action.

HIGH PRIEST: Never for one moment.

HEROD: Well, the Council was decades ago. Get on like a house on fire with the clergy these days, don't I? Especially our High Priest. You help me maintain that harmonious balance of our interests. For the sake of the people. Confound them. And finding your replacement would be too much work at my age: candidates, lobbying, petitions. I think I'll keep you.

HIGH PRIEST: I rejoice. Your majesty is a fountain of hilarity.

HEROD: Yes, I have my moments. No, no, you tuck in; munch away.

HIGH PRIEST: You wanted to see me, your majesty?

HEROD: Ah, yes. Well, your Grace...it's, ah...it's that time of year again.

HIGH PRIEST: Oh. The, er...

HEROD: The anniversary.

HIGH PRIEST: Of the - incident. Yes, of course, the incident. Does your majesty feel any easier as regards dealing with it this year?

HEROD: Can't say I do.

HIGH PRIEST: The mothers will have forgotten by now – well, not *forgotten*, not actually forgotten, but the sting will be greatly diminished. The immediacy of emotion will be gone. In some cases. I imagine. Time is a great healer. And, of course –

HEROD: I know: it was only eight.

HIGH PRIEST: Possibly only seven. Apparently one was not too badly affected and survived. The soldier was unenthusiastic.

HEROD: That doesn't change anything.

HIGH PRIEST: Then, sire, I repeat what I said last year: you must see this in the light of logic and morality. What else could you have done? As you have just said, stability, unity, security. You recall the three Persian ambassadors? You remember their words?

HEROD: 'Where is he that is born King of the Jews?'

HIGH PRIEST: Exactly. They believed an heir had been born to you in this palace, their reasons unclear except that they interpreted the appearance of a new star, which you yourself had not seen –

HEROD: I wasn't looking.

HIGH PRIEST: Of course. And you summoned myself and the senior rabbis to settle what I could call the theological dimension.

HEROD: 'King of the Jews' means 'Messiah', doesn't it? That's theological.

HIGH PRIEST: Well, God's, er, chosen king, yes. In the minds of many. And when we informed you from the prophets that this figure was to appear in Bethlehem, you chose to believe the prophets in this respect and...took reasonable precautions.

HEROD: Yes, and I even consulted you. You heard me give the order. I remember it all.

HIGH PRIEST: Then reflect on it and assure yourself that you probably spared your people a bitter and useless war. You can imagine the reaction of Rome if some hothead attempted to topple your regime by announcing he had found the new king in Bethlehem? But you wisely made sure there was no 'new king' to be found. Pre-emptive wisdom, sire. True, you could not, with certainty, target a single individual, but knowing the age range, you realised you could avert thousands of casualties by allowing only eight. Or seven. No, your majesty, you guaranteed stability and safety by safeguarding your regime. There was no choice, sire. The country is in fact in your debt.

HEROD: Impeccable logic. No doubt history will prove you correct. Well, thank you for coming. I'm sure you'll want to get back to the banquet.

HIGH PRIEST: Only too happy to serve. Good night, sire.

HEROD: I wish you hadn't said 'probably'.

HIGH PRIEST: Your majesty, allow me to say that you of all people have had the opportunity to observe first-hand what the Roman war machine is capable of. Many believe me theologically liberal, but I am convinced that the appearance of a Messiah at this time would tear this nation and its history in two. It is the last thing we want. Thus far, you have protected us from it. Frankly, sire, you'd do it again. And you'd be right. Good night, sire.

(HIGH PRIEST exits. TIMON enters and busies himself.)

TIMON: You shouldn't play with him like that, y'know.

HEROD: He represents my detestable subjects. I feel I get my own back. You shouldn't be listening anyway.

TIMON: I always listen when it's the High Priest – you might need me, you get yourself into such a lather at times. You needed the Green Bottle once, remember?

HEROD: He's a cold fish. A walking brain. I never met such a logical man in my life. He must have been brought up by statues.

TIMON: Sire, you're not going to marry Lady Zibeah, are you?

HEROD: My heart doesn't leap at the prospect, Timon, but consider the practical issues. An aristocratic Jewish wife would help my position with the people. A shrewd thinker by my side would be no bad thing. And there might be sons.

TIMON: But you've got sons.

HEROD: Wastrels. Plotters. They look out for themselves. Antipater's the worst: I think the people hate him more than me.

TIMON: That reminds me: the guard's been waiting with the prison report. About Antipater.

HEROD: Oh. Well, let's find out how he's lowering the tone down there.

(TIMON beckons off and the GUARD enters.)

Now then. What do you have to tell me?

GUARD: Sire, the Prince is comfortable –

HEROD: More than he deserves. What else?

GUARD: He's very quiet, Sire. Asked me to express his gratitude for your choice of leg-irons. Says they're not too heavy.

HEROD: Well, watch him. He's not to be trusted. Here, give him this. There's some chicken legs and a couple of larks' tongues. I won't give you wine, you'll drink it on the way. Tell him I'll visit him next week if he behaves himself.

GUARD: Sire, permit me to say…I'm very moved.

(GUARD exits.)

TIMON: You don't think Antipater would sort of...reform, do you?

HEROD: Not a chance. No more than the rest of them. But there's a surprise coming: the dynasty ends with me. I'm dividing the kingdom up – they can have a piece each, it's in my will already. I'm the last King of the Jews. Unless...

TIMON: Sire?

HEROD: Unless there was...some little boy. A new heir, the first of a new line...

TIMON: The dynasty would go on.

HEROD: And the people would accept him, you see, if he had that Jewish mother from the old royal line. Though there'll be no tears when I go.

(TIMON looks struck. HEROD pauses.)

You can come in now. Come on, come on, get in.

(ZIBEAH nervously enters.)

I told you I miss nothing: the curtain twitching, the door edging open. How long have you been there?

ZIBEAH: I was waiting for your majesty's summons.

HEROD: If you and I are to get anywhere, you won't lie to me. And in any case I'll make no decision while your husband's alive: I'm not so tasteless. Now, come over here. Sit down. I suppose you heard all that?

ZIBEAH: I could not help but hear – *(Warning glance from Herod.)* Your majesty spoke of the dynasty. You were gracious enough to consider that I –

HEROD: Stop talking like a Roman monument! You're not reading the minutes of the Senate, you know. Talk to me like a real person. So, you heard me? All right, down to business: I suppose you're in a position to reproduce?

ZIBEAH: I – er – yes.

HEROD: But you don't have any children. Why not?

ZIBEAH: Uzzah didn't want any. He said he was too busy.

HEROD: Well, it only needs ten minutes now and again. How busy could he be? Finance on the brain. All right, children a distinct possibility. *(Peers appraisingly.)* Good legs under that Roman horse-blanket. Wouldn't you say, Timon? Never mind, they'll still be there on the honeymoon. Now, stand up. No, I'd want you more statuesque. Chin up, shoulders back. Breeding's not everything: you have to look the part. Makeup's overdone; you look like a Celtic chieftain. Well, I suppose there's nothing that can't be modified. Or hidden. *(Zibeah affronted.)* And with everything else taken into account, the arrangement is...not impossible.

ZIBEAH: Timon! Is he mad?

TIMON: No!

HEROD: Well, we ought to get to know each other a little better – some enlightening conversation, eh? Timon, did I ever tell you how I became King of the Jews?

TIMON: Frequently.

ZIBEAH: I'd love to hear that.

HEROD: Now, you're not just saying that?

ZIBEAH: No, really, I'm fascinated.

HEROD: Oh, all right, then. Cast your mind back thirty-five years – the Roman world in turmoil, decades of civil war. Great men arise – Caesar, Brutus, Anthony – the power struggles are endless. Meanwhile, General Pompey has occupied this little land of Judaea and brought it into the empire. Who impresses the Romans but the Herod family? The youngest son is particularly outstanding, a vigorous commander and tactician: he is deployed to pacify the bandits in the north. Soon he amasses power and wealth and becomes a great man in the kingdom. We were Idumeans, of course, not Jewish at all, but we were the leaders Rome wanted.

ZIBEAH: That would be before you were king, before Mariamne.

HEROD: What? *(Zibeah realises she has said the wrong thing.)*

ZIBEAH: Before...Mariamne.

HEROD: Don't mention that whore to me! The stink of her adulteries sickened me! She forsook me, she plotted with her lovers to bring me down. But I wreaked justice on her –

TIMON: Now. Justice on who?

HEROD: On – on her. That woman, the queen.

TIMON: Oh dear, it looks as if your stomach's got the collywobbles. Have a little sip of this.

HEROD: Ah. Thank you, Timon. Yes, the queen. Mariamne...

TIMON: Mariamne lives in Egypt now, remember? A long way away, and she's been there for a long, long time.

HEROD: Yes, of course. Silly of me. What was I saying? What was I saying, Timon? Oh, so long ago, so far away. So much done and I can't remember, I can't remember my life. I don't even know if it mattered. Tell me, Timon. Tell me it matters that I'm alive.

Act Two: Beyond Bottles.

(Spotlight on TIMON. He speaks to the audience.)

TIMON: Imagine it! Herod the Great, the most powerful and feared king in Asia, manipulated by that ambitious woman Zibeah of ben Sirach. With her own husband so ill he had only days left, she was determined to marry Herod and took advantage of his age and wandering wits. And I, Timon Athenagoras, what could I do? I was only Herod's personal servant, but I stood by him. In his sickness, he launched into his favourite story – the one about how he became king.

(Lights up: the group take up where they left off.)

HEROD: What was I saying? What was I saying, Timon? Oh, so long ago, so far away. So much done and I can't remember, I can't remember my life. I don't even know if it mattered. Tell me, Timon. Tell me it matters that I'm alive.

TIMON: It matters very much. You were telling us how you got to be king.

ZIBEAH: The Herods were the leaders Rome wanted.

HEROD: Ah, yes. That's it: the leaders Rome wanted.

ZIBEAH: How wonderful! To be a finger on the hand of the world's mightiest empire!

HEROD: A what? I say, that's rather good. A finger on the hand... Yes, I like that; fine turn of phrase. Timon, write that down. Are you literary, my dear?

ZIBEAH: I have read a fair amount.

HEROD: You read too? Even better.

ZIBEAH: Yes. I hope one day to read a great chronicle: Rome and Herod.

HEROD: Herod and Rome sounds better.

ZIBEAH: Of course. But you were saying?

HEROD: Was I?

TIMON: Becoming king. It's Cleopatra next. *(To Zibeah)* Zibeah…you're learning fast, dear.

HEROD: Ah, Cleopatra. The jewel of the Nile. Well, the power struggles got worse and everybody looked for allies. First Caesar had his wild affair with Cleopatra, then got hacked to bits for being too popular. And then Anthony, that absurd boyfriend of hers, pulled me into it and I fought for the coalition between him and Egypt. Of course he and the Senate had already recognised my abilities and appointed me king.

TIMON: Ta-daah!

HEROD: Thank you Timon, I believe I can manage. Now I've lost the thread. Where was I?

ZIBEAH: The Senate appointed you king.

HEROD: Ah yes; but then a new figure arose – Augustus, the complete man: leader, tactician, economist, reformer. He beat down the opposition till it was a contest between him and that doomed couple, with the whole Roman world the prize. It hung on one battle by sea at Actium. Cleopatra sent her heavy old Egyptian tubs against those deadly Roman galleys. She hadn't a chance: she turned and fled. Anthony was killed soon after and then she killed herself rather than live without him. An incurable romantic to the end. Strange and awesome it was to see such beauty destroy itself.

ZIBEAH *(Fascinated)*: But – where did that leave you?

HEROD: Up the Nile without a paddle. Augustus was now master of the world and I had fought for his enemies.

ZIBEAH: What did you do?

HEROD: What I do best. I brazened it out: I imposed my will on the situation.

ZIBEAH: But how?

HEROD: Very simple: realism, flattery, money.

ZIBEAH: I don't quite follow.

HEROD: Well, I went to Augustus and gave him a present: a massive pile of hard cash – out of sheer respect, of course: practically bankrupted the country. Then I made this tremendous speech about how wonderful it was that he was now in charge of the civilised world and how clever he was to have managed it – Romans love that sort of thing.

ZIBEAH: And realism?

HEROD: Just admitted the facts, then used them. I told him yes, absolutely true, I'd served his enemies – and, what's more, I'd been the best. But, I said, take me on and I'll be the best for you, and better. And he looked at me like an eagle that's just eaten it's prey and isn't sure if it's still hungry.

ZIBEAH: And – it worked?

HEROD: It worked. I've never taken a bigger risk before or since, but it worked. It wasn't just the money – I meant it, every word, and he could see that. So for a long, sweating moment we looked each other in the eye, and then he broke and laughed. 'Well, my new friend,' he said, 'you can look after Judaea for me. You can be my King of the Jews.' Thirty years later, here I am. Here I *am.*

(TIMON and Zibeah applaud.)

ZIBEAH: Bravo! Absolute triumph! Aren't you clever!

HEROD: Yes, and I can tell you no king would more willingly have lined his subjects up and strangled them one by one.

ZIBEAH: Oh dear.

HEROD: Oh dear indeed. Since the day I was crowned, I've had to fight them as much as rule them.

ZIBEAH: They've never had a greater king. They just don't know it.

HEROD: Understatement of the year. I'm not Jewish, so they've never accepted me, except for a little while, for Mariamne's sake. They've criticised and whined about everything I've done for them. I adorned the cities with magnificent buildings: they resented the expense; I made the kingdom ring with fame throughout the world: they resented the Romans in the civil service; I gave them stunning theatres and circuses: they said I paid Greek athletes with Jewish money. Who could rule these people?

ZIBEAH: You could. You have. A lesser man would have been swept away.

HEROD: I feel your passion, Zibeah of ben Sirach. Your heart swells at these tales of mastery and domination.

ZIBEAH: A kindred spirit, Herod. There's a joy in power.

HEROD: Yes, and in mutual understanding: a joint unveiling. One knows one is not alone.

(Each of them considers this, eyes locked, till Herod changes the mood.)

Well, I wish I'd had more joy in power. The wretches never thought I could do anything right.

TIMON: There was the Temple.

HEROD: The Temple. Yes, my greatest project. They were worshipping in a five hundred-year-old ruin and I gave them a magnificent shrine, the most beautiful building in Asia: the blazing white carrara marble, the Holy Place overlaid with gold. Travellers on the hill in the morning sun couldn't look at it: it shone and burned like the cherubim. The colonnades in flawless proportion, the work on the furnishings perfect: the altar, the great candlestick, the golden skillet engraved with the divine name... *(He breaks off and his mood darkens.)* A quintessence of stone. Hearts of stone. Hard, bloodless gold. Iron power: sharp, unbending. *(He pauses.)* I must leave you for a moment, I have someone to see. Timon, will you attend to the lady Zibeah's needs?

(HEROD exits.)

ZIBEAH: What happened there? I thought he was enjoying that speech.

TIMON: Can't say.

ZIBEAH: I think you can. Let's hear it.

TIMON: Are you going to be polite?

ZIBEAH: Well, how's this? Let's make a little coalition – I'll be Cleopatra, you be Anthony. True lovers can't hide anything from each other, so come on. What's his problem with the Temple?

TIMON: Well, it was going to win the hearts of his people back to him.

ZIBEAH: The hearts of his people are a million miles from him.

TIMON: It had to be something stupendous, you see.

ZIBEAH: All those thoughtful, deeply-felt assassinations weren't enough?

TIMON: Well it worked. You must have been in the Temple, you know what it's like.

ZIBEAH: Yes, and it didn't collapse when I walked in. Quite a place.

TIMON: They loved him for it, they really did. His worst critics suddenly hadn't a word to say against him. Nobody could praise him enough – everything changed.

ZIBEAH: And then?

TIMON: He added a finishing touch. He put a Roman eagle over the door.

ZIBEAH: Not very clever.

TIMON: If people wanted to go in to sacrifice or just listen to the prayers they had to walk beneath that big pagan eagle. They hated it: it ruined everything.

ZIBEAH: A reminder of realities: you think God's in charge, but really it's Rome.

TIMON: Should you say that? I mean, you're Jewish!

ZIBEAH: I don't see any thunderbolts. Why did he do it?

TIMON: Nobody knew. Something to please the emperor maybe. They make a sacrifice for him every day, so Herod might've thought they wouldn't mind the eagle.

ZIBEAH: A sacrifice *for* the emperor, not *to* the emperor. Even he knows how far he can go.

TIMON: Well, they protested, they rioted, but the eagle stayed. Herod wouldn't move it.

ZIBEAH: Very subtle: Rome might be in charge, but the real issue's Herod's authority.

TIMON: You might have a point. The eagle came down not long ago: a lot of angry young men had had enough one day and hacked it off the wall. Instant heroes.

ZIBEAH: Yes, I heard about that. They got a fair trial, though, didn't they?

TIMON: And they were burned alive very fairly too. It was all just nasty. Herod lost everything he'd gained. And maybe one more son. They say Prince Antipater was behind the riots.

ZIBEAH: So much for the Temple. Rather sounds as if Herod got God and Augustus mixed up.

TIMON: Mixed up?

ZIBEAH: He brazened it out with both of them: gave them tremendous gifts but took a risk as well.

TIMON: Meaning…?

ZIBEAH: He tested them both. He'd actually been Augustus' enemy, and with God he'd been...well, not among the righteous, shall we say. 'Augustus, here's some money, overlook me fighting you. God, here's a Temple, overlook my murders. And if there's any Roman deities listening, here's a nice eagle. Hope you don't mind, God.' Rather pushing it, don't you think?

TIMON: Sounds a bit complicated.

ZIBEAH: Oh, it's terribly deep, darling. Don't you worry your loyal head about it. But it's all so exciting, isn't it?

TIMON: You love this stuff.

ZIBEAH: It's my nature; and another reason to marry Herod. He's surrounded by the most marvellous fun. I'm so terribly angry at Uzzah sometimes. For being so boring, and for dying so slowly. But things are going to change.

(HEROD enters.)

Ah, Herod. Welcome back.

HEROD: My dear, could you find some more powder for that nose of yours? Another interview.

ZIBEAH: Of course. And this time, no peeking. Oh Herod, I am so thrilled.

HEROD: Timon, perhaps you could just – be in the room. The High Priest again. I hoped those white stones would be enough, but how can one judge? How can I know you're even aware of me? How can I know you're even there?

TIMON: What?

HEROD: Nothing, nothing.

TIMON: Sire, the High Priest...

HIGH PRIEST: Your majesty?

HEROD: Ah, hello again. Kind of you to come, Your Grace. I - I wished to continue –

HIGH PRIEST: Your majesty appears burdened.

HEROD: It's not working.

HIGH PRIEST: I failed to bring solace. I am most sorry.

HEROD: Oh, you rationalised the whole thing perfectly. Sensible, logical, politically astute, even flattering. It's just not working. I don't…feel any better.

HIGH PRIEST: How may I ease your majesty?

HEROD: I wish I knew. Come to think of it, you were pretty calm at the time. You've been pretty calm ever since. Every year I drag it all up again and you never turn a hair. What's your secret?

HIGH PRIEST: Well, of course I was one step removed from the event –

HEROD: You were in the middle of it. You knew what I was doing! You knew it!

HIGH PRIEST: Well, in the light of the probabilities –

HEROD: You could have argued me out of it! You could have intervened with the military, bribed the commander. I'd never have known.

HIGH PRIEST: Your own express order –

HEROD: A vague report six months later, that would have satisfied me. You knew that.

HIGH PRIEST: I have failed to please. Forgive me, sire.

HEROD: Well, please me now. What's your secret?

HIGH PRIEST: My secret?

HEROD: What do Jews do when they can't let go? I'm going to say that word: what do you do with your conscience?

HIGH PRIEST: Ah. The discussion has changed its emphasis this year.

HEROD: Don't toy with me. I'm talking about guilt – yours and mine. Don't deny it.

HIGH PRIEST: Well, sire, we have sacrifice.

HEROD: I know that. Even the Romans sacrifice: they placate those gods of theirs. Is that what you mean?

HIGH PRIEST: No sire. God is unshakeably on our side already.

HEROD: What do you have to do for that?

HIGH PRIEST: That's simply how it is.

HEROD: All right, you kill something on an altar and that's it.

HIGH PRIEST: Broadly speaking. Traditional values would say the person searches his heart.

HEROD: Searches his heart?

HIGH PRIEST: Well, penitence, admission of guilt – the unreflective view. I don't want to be theological.

HEROD: Be theological.

HIGH PRIEST: Well, to quote the Psalms, 'Clean hands and a pure heart.' The popular view, as I'm sure you know, thrives on this – without the benefit of theological reading and reflection, of course, but the idea is that the worshipper does go through the customary rituals, such as cleansing his hands, but must be inwardly 'clean' – a metaphor for pure motives, pure attitude towards God, sorrow for one's sins –

HEROD: I haven't had a pure motive for thirty years. I *love* my sins. What are you telling me?

HIGH PRIEST: Well, I would say that is the symbol of the guilt sacrifice: not some mechanical antidote for guilt, but an encouragement, a pointer to a higher intent, to integrity.

HEROD: Integrity. The man who allowed the assassination of children is talking to me about integrity. You really think this kingdom is run on integrity?

HIGH PRIEST: Ah. Theology shades into politics: almost a paradigm shift –

HEROD: Look at him! He's warming to the discussion! Which debating society will you try it on?

HIGH PRIEST: Your majesty, no. I speak as between intelligent men.

HEROD: And are you going to tell me God is so much on your side he would thank you and I for butchering eight children to save the nation?

HIGH PRIEST: Very stark language, sire, but an intellectual case could be made –

HEROD: Intellectual? You think those mothers in Bethlehem were intellectuals? Perhaps a dissertation in Political Science would explain it all for them. 'Well, you see, my dear, the murder of your little boy served the state and was perfectly logical. Let me go through it with you step by step.' 'Oh, is that what it's about? I see it all now – silly of me to be so upset.'

HIGH PRIEST: Your majesty, your own express order –

HEROD: Which you should have countermanded!

HIGH PRIEST: Sire, I cannot say this strongly enough: put it out of your mind. I commend to you my own belief that preoccupation with the idea of objective guilt and its emotions belongs to a very early stage of religious development – the intellectual nursery, if you will. We have moved on, we have developed.

HEROD: Moved on?

HIGH PRIEST: We are adults now, and recognise moral freedom. Our morality is personal – we define it, we shape it, ourselves. You seek my help as a religious leader: that is it. Free yourself from small thinking, sire, and peace will eventually come. It is the reasonable view; and it works, intellectually and politically. You used it years ago to protect our nation – how could I have intervened?

HEROD: You really believe all that?

HIGH PRIEST: Certainly. I'm a thinking man.

HEROD: But you lead the sacrifices and prayers for thousands of people. You teach your Torah, you inform the synagogues.

HIGH PRIEST: Of course I do: I'm the High Priest.

HEROD: No, no, it's too real, the guilt's too real. It's part of me, it's who I am: a guilty man. I can't deny it, not if I'm sane. But I was forced into it - I was troubled, I was ill. Persian diplomats questioning my power base. I couldn't be expected to act normally. It would have been different, and you should have realised that. You forced me into my guilt, you let me run headlong. You took your own guilt and piled it on me. Why should I tolerate you any longer? You bring the thing before my eyes constantly. I can't look at you but I remember –

TIMON: Sire? Sire, I think perhaps a little sip from the green bottle –

HEROD: I don't want the green bottle! You're all the same with your smooth words and your damned medicines. Keep the old fool quiet, talk him down, keep him drugged. Well, I don't need you. I understand power, I understand control. Bethlehem kept me here and here I'll stay, with you or without you. Survive with Herod or leave him and be broken. Take your sides, make your choice, I won't wait much longer.

(HEROD exits.)

TIMON: He's not having a good day. He didn't mean all that.

HIGH PRIEST: I've heard it all before. I should keep that green bottle handy if I were you.

(HIGH PRIEST begins to leave.)

TIMON: Er, Your Grace? Your Grace, sir, can I ask you something?

HIGH PRIEST: I'm waiting.

TIMON: Well, it's, er, sort of difficult, because, well – you know I'm not Jewish?

HIGH PRIEST: Nobody's perfect.

TIMON: Yes, but what I mean is – it's a question about God, sir, and you're an expert, aren't you? I mean, you're sort of head Jew, aren't you? And of course I'm Greek.

HIGH PRIEST: Then why are you asking me?

TIMON: Well, our gods aren't what you'd call…they're not *involved*, sir. Nobody knows if they listen to you or not. And they don't behave any better than anybody else, not if you believe the stories.

HIGH PRIEST: Your point being?

TIMON: It's just – I suppose I'd like a better god than that. And, er, I sort of like what your rabbis say about God, what I've heard anyway –

HIGH PRIEST: And your question?

TIMON *(Hesitates, then abruptly)*: Does God bother with you if you're not Jewish? Would he listen? Would he get involved with you?

HIGH PRIEST: Is this a personal interest? Or a matter of theory?

TIMON: Well, it's…it's very interesting. My uncle was a philosopher, you know.

HIGH PRIEST: Really? Well, God is the God of all nations, whatever the philosophers may say, and they are all as a drop in a bucket to him. I'm not speaking about ethics now, you understand. I'm referring to God's reality, his universality, the exclusivity of his intentions. But in theory he may be attentive to a gentile.

TIMON: Well – for example?

HIGH PRIEST: Examples. Well, the prophet Elijah was sent to the aid of an indigenous dweller in Zarephath, by no means a Jewish region. He also witnessed God cure a pagan general of leprosy – without condoning his paganism, you understand – and God also initiated the campaigns of the pagan general Cyrus in order to liberate us from Babylonian oppression. I could go on, but the matter is certainly open.

TIMON: Ah. Well, that's very helpful, Your Grace.

HIGH PRIEST: And as you know, our Temple has a large court around the sacred areas specifically designed as a venue for non-Jews to approach God.

TIMON:. Oh, yes. And what if I went into the sacred bits?

HIGH PRIEST: We would kill you. Was there anything else?

TIMON: No. No, thank you very much.

HIGH PRIEST: Then it's back to the banquet for me. Remember the green bottle.

TIMON: Thank you *very* much. Well, I'll have to do this myself. How do you get a god – er – how do you get *God* to listen to you? Because he's got to; I'm so worried, he's got to. Oh, I don't know. Oh, here goes. I, um, I do approach thee in reverent fear. Er – oh, hang on, you're supposed to cover your head. I don't think that's how they do it. Oh, never mind. Um – I approach thee and I know that thou art Jewish and I art not, but I do beseech thee that thou wilt be attentive unto my cry and that I am doing this properly so that thou wilt, er, be attentive. And listen. And, er, rise up…from thy…majestic dwelling place, and – and – and I don't have a clue how to do this and I don't know what you say to make it work and I just – can't pray. I can talk but I can't pray, so I hope you listen to people just talking and – and – talking about what's on their minds and there's certainly nothing religious on my mind, so I hope that's all right – it'll have to be all right, I can't do anything about it – and actually I'm doing this because I'm worried sick about Herod, really worried, because he's just a sick old man and he's not got long to go and nobody cares about him and…I love him. Nobody else does, just me. I don't care what he's done,

I really love him, and I don't want him to die all guilty and full of pain and not one person near him that cares about him. I'd like him to know that at least I do. I just wanted to say that. I don't know what you could do about it, the guilt and all. He hasn't got a bottle for guilt. Well, there you are. I – I feel listened to. Very funny, it's like the feeling you get when somebody takes you seriously. I didn't expect that at all. Well, I'm finished, I think, so, er, back to work – oh!

HEROD: Praying, Timon?

TIMON: Oh. Oh, sire. I hope you don't mind but I just had to –

HEROD: I am perfectly sane. My thoughts at this moment are of purest crystal. If prayer grants clarity I have it now. What if it were decided that, in spite of everything, in spite of all the deeds of your life, all would be well. And this not earned or won, simply granted. If one wanted it. You might call it mercy.

(HEROD pauses and seems to wander somewhat.)

What are you staring at? Never seen an old man before?

TIMON: I was – I was praying, sort of. I think. For you. Is that all right?

HEROD: Strange that I of all people should seize upon the idea of mercy. I've never been merciful in my life.

TIMON: You've been a great king –

HEROD: One would have to want it of course. If I pardon a criminal and he insists on throwing himself on the executioner's sword nonetheless even though I'm holding out mercy to him, how can he receive it? We must want, we must accept it. Since we are as we are, it must work that way. Timon, a clear mind brings its pains: one knows things, one remembers. I have no madness to cushion me at this moment, no fragmented psyche in which to lose my memories. I see all my deeds and all my motives. You would not know, Timon, that when I went to bow before Augustus, knowing I might not come back, I thought jealously of my Mariamne. Whose would she be, if my head rolled at Augustus' feet?

I could not stand it: if I could not have her, no-one would. I left orders that if I did not return she was to be killed.

TIMON: But you did return.

HEROD: Yes, and as time went by I enjoyed her and forgot. Ironic that a Roman saved her.

TIMON: Well, then...?

HEROD: She found out. Somehow she found out. She was furious, she forsook my bed. And then my wild fear flared up. I accused her, I dragged her to trial, I made her mother bear false witness against her, and I sentenced her to die. She was so very brave when she heard the sentence, but my hatred lasted till her breath had gone and then I loved her again. And I love her still.

TIMON: You were wrong, you know. When you said there'll be no tears when you die. There'll be mine.

HEROD: Timon. Timon, please listen to me. I want to say -

ZIBEAH: I though he'd never go. What does anybody find to talk about with the High Priest? Our local rabbi's bad enough, but he's boring and sweet – the H.P. makes you feel as if there's a block of ice on your head. A large empty space forms round him at the banquet. But how is my stimulating, controversial Herod?

HEROD: Preoccupied.

ZIBEAH: Oh? With what?

HEROD: You wouldn't understand.

ZIBEAH: You're all right, aren't you?

HEROD: Well, I'm not so sure. Timon, what was I saying? I'm feeling rather anxious: I haven't written to Mariamne for a long time and I think I've lost Cleopatra's address. She'll think I don't care anymore. Even the High Priest doesn't know where Cleopatra lives.

TIMON: Well, shall we have a nice seat and finish our supper and perhaps we'll remember?

HEROD: I could always send it to Cleopatra, care of Egypt: that should get it. Everybody knows her in Egypt –

TIMON: Well let's just –

HEROD: Zibeah, I don't know if I'm up to this marriage thing. My age, my health...

TIMON: That's right, don't rush into it.

ZIBEAH: But it's so promising! You'll feel differently tomorrow.

HEROD: I'm really sort of going off the idea. I mean, what's the point, what's the point of anything? You want things and they don't come to you, things you need –

TIMON: What you need is a rest and your supper, so come on, old king, let's be having you -

HEROD: Oh! My chest! Timon, quick! Red bottle, red bottle.

TIMON: Here you are, take it quick.

HEROD: It's not working! Green bottle!

TIMON: Not the Green Bottle!

HEROD: Green Bottle, Timon!

TIMON: There. Is that all right? Is it working?

HEROD: No, no, where's the yellow one?

TIMON: You threw it at the doctor.

ZIBEAH: Wait a minute! You're not saying - ? You can't be –

HEROD: Sorry to disappoint you, my dear. Back to the provinces, eh?

ZIBEAH: It must be a false alarm. Everybody has them.

HEROD: Now you mention it, I've had one a week on average for the last five years.

ZIBEAH: Noble Herod, you should not end thus.

HEROD: What? Are you drunk?

ZIBEAH: Are you going to just fizzle out? What about the dynasty? What about the sons that should follow you?

HEROD: I've got sons that'll follow me.

ZIBEAH: Not those wasters! Real sons, men worthy of their father – er, er – new sons altogether. A glorious line of kings stretching into the future, sprung from your loins.

HEROD: I think my loins have rather had their day –

ZIBEAH: *What about the dynasty?* Are you going to just throw it all away?

HEROD: Ah yes, the dynasty. Well, I suppose I might owe it to the nation, to my people –

ZIBEAH: No you don't! You can't stand your people! You don't owe them anything. You owe it to yourself – you're the meanest, most conniving, heartless old swine that ever sat on the throne of this country and you got yourself there and you're going to stay there and then your descendants are going to rule this place forever!

HEROD: Don't I need a queen for that?

ZIBEAH: Yes! A wife! Take a wife!

HEROD: Ah... *(Wandered.)* Have you seen my wife? She must be very –

ZIBEAH: Marry me! Marry me now! I'm the woman for you! You know I am. All your other wives were small-time schemers, but I'm big enough for you, Herod the Great. I'm strong enough, I'm arrogant enough, I've got all of the gifts and none of the scruples. I'll whip your people into shape, I'll lash them with scorpions, I'll assassinate whoever it takes –

HEROD: You can't rush these things –

ZIBEAH: There's nothing like a short engagement. Send your little tragedy queen for the High Priest: just a little private wedding and we'll be king and queen in ten minutes flat. Then we can start on the dynasty.

HEROD: My state of health...

ZIBEAH: You'll be around for a week at least. Marry me, Herod, and I'll give you triplets with the first delivery!

HEROD: Triplets in a week? You'll finish me off!

ZIBEAH: Oh, come on, Herod! The state my husband's in you'll probably only be a bigamist for half an hour.

HEROD: Well, I, er –

ZIBEAH: Think proudly of the sons I will bear you, those future kings. Imagine them in your arms, imagine their first steps.

HEROD: My children. In my arms. *(He pauses, then, quietly:)* I'll do it. I'll marry you, Zibeah.

ZIBEAH: My love! What years of joy lie ahead! Come to my arms!

HEROD: Well, we'd better get the invitations sent out. See to that, Timon. Remember to invite Cleopatra. I don't suppose she'll come this time either.

TIMON: They keep her terribly busy in Egypt.

HEROD: Ask the Emperor, then. He just sleeps all day. We'll get a better present, too.

TIMON: Persian ambassador?

HEROD: No, great fat fool, he wouldn't be interested. Besides, he's a eunuch: inappropriate for weddings.

ZIBEAH: Well, I'll make up a little guest list of my own.

HEROD: You could always invite your husband.

ZIBEAH: What wit, my love!

HEROD: Well, just a little technicality. He is alive, you know.

ZIBEAH: Well, if he doesn't go soon, I'll divorce him. You can get it rushed through the courts, can't you?

HEROD: Make a note, Timon. Of course, the news of his sudden divorce may hasten your current spouse's passing.

ZIBEAH: There you are: it works both ways.

TIMON: Will you be asking the Proconsul, sire?

ZIBEAH: Absolutely not! His wife's an absolute cow. Do you know what she said to me?

HEROD: Can you give me a clue?

TIMON: But definitely the Emperor?

HEROD: Let me consult. My dear, will you give the absolute ruler of the entire civilised world permission to attend your wedding?

ZIBEAH: Well, we'll have to keep in with him, won't we? I don't want you deposed or anything.

HEROD: I think I could say I have job security. What's more, I believe the Empress is charming – Ah, general Nabal. Just in time to hear the happy news.

NABAL: What news, sire?

ZIBEAH: We're engaged! Or we will be when we get things sorted out.

HEROD: Her husband.

NABAL: Ah. In that case, your majesty, I ask permission to address the lady Zibeah.

HEROD: Don't mind me; I'm just the king.

ZIBEAH: Nabal, you do choose your moments. What is it?

NABAL: Important news, Zibeah. About Uzzah. I've come to break it to you: your months of waiting have come to an end.

ZIBEAH: An end? You mean - ?

NABAL: Yes, that long and terrible sickness is over at last.

ZIBEAH: You mean he's gone? He's dead?

HEROD: My deepest condolences.

ZIBEAH: Oh, never mind that –

HEROD: I'm not talking to you; you don't need condolences. General, my sympathy on the loss of your brother. A finer financial brain I never knew. Appallingly boring of course, but I find that's an advantage for a financial official. So when I appointed him –

NABAL: Your majesty, I must tell you the situation is not what it appears.

HEROD: What is it then?

ZIBEAH: Never mind the situation. There's probably nobody left up there that can count. Herod, don't you see? We're free – legally, morally –

HEROD: Hasn't bothered you so far.

ZIBEAH: Well, it *looks* better. But we can be king and queen tonight.

HEROD: You could at least get the death certificate. The messenger might have it.

ZIBEAH: Of course. Nabal, where's the messenger? I want to reward him for bringing the good news: my first act as queen.

NABAL: I doubt it, Zibeah. *(Calls off.)* You can come in now!

(MESSENGER enters. He wears a hood.)

ZIBEAH: Well, I'm glad to see you. Congratulations. *(Removes the hood.)* Uzzah!

UZZAH: Congratulations *are* in order, my dear. I'm not dead!

HEROD: I wish you'd make up your mind. It's very confusing.

NABAL: All will be made clear, sire.

HEROD: Well, look, your husband's recovered. Give him a kiss or something.

ZIBEAH: Darling. How wonderful –

UZZAH: Don't bother with the kiss, Zibeah. It wouldn't be very meaningful.

ZIBEAH: Dearest –

NABAL: It's over, Zibeah. We found the poison. The old woman who supplied it to you confessed.

UZZAH: No wonder you insisted on giving me my medicine yourself. Tiny drops of poison in every dose to make it look like a long, lingering illness. Scorpion sting distilled in the venom of twelve different Egyptian spiders. With a dash of honey. To think you were feeding me that for six months.

HEROD: That was very foolish. You could have done it in five minutes with strychnine.

UZZAH: You were too confident, Zibeah. You slipped up when you came down here and left the old woman to administer the poison. She dropped a jar of the undiluted stuff in the street. Two camels licked it up and dropped dead.. So we examined my so-called medicine. We tried it on grasshoppers: they turned blue and burst . And then there was your jewel box with the false bottom and jars of the concentrated poison inside. I discontinued treatment, of course, and we encouraged the old lady to give us a fast-working antidote. And so here I am.

NABAL: A sorry but conclusive tale. Your majesty, with your permission, I will remove this woman from your presence. Guards!

(Guards enter: Zibeah is seized.)

Now's your chance, Zibeah. Beg for mercy. His majesty may be gracious.

ZIBEAH: No, I won't. I choose my dignity. My strength, my self-determination. Mercy would make me someone I'm not. Ah, Herod. I could have made you such a wife.

HEROD: Have you seen my wife...?

TIMON: General, sir, time to go, I think.

(All exit except HEROD and TIMON.)

TIMON: Well, all our guests have gone. It's just you and me. Will you be wanting your sleeping potion now?

HEROD: Yes, it was a lovely evening. I do like chatting with people. Wasn't there a lady, a nice lady? Oh dear, who was that? Was it my wife, Timon? Was my wife here?

TIMON: No, she's in Egypt, remember? She lives with Cleopatra now.

HEROD: Oh, yes. Did you ever find Cleopatra's address?

TIMON: Oh, I think she's moved. She's in a great big square house with a point at the top.

HEROD: Really? She must have marvellous banquets.

TIMON: I don't think she gets many visitors.

HEROD: Her house was very busy when I knew her. Roman generals coming and going, Nubians with leopards on chains, girls dancing with beautiful headdresses made of perfumed beeswax and when they danced the wax melted and the most wonderful fragrances would fill the room. And when Cleopatra was carried in no-one would speak. She stepped down from her litter and crossed the floor like a gazelle. She wore miraculous garments like gossamer spun from gold and finest silk. You could see through some of them. And then she would settle on those huge crimson pillows and look round at everyone with jaguar's eyes. She beckoned to me and I lay on the bolster beside her. 'Herod of Jewry,' she said, 'tell me of your land.' 'Jewel of Egypt,' I said, 'I cannot, for to sit by you is to be silent.' She smiled and pierced my heart. 'Then we will meet again,' she whispered, 'and then perhaps you will speak to me.' And speak I did: there were not enough words in me to tell my heart to Cleopatra. We would stand on the harbour at Alexandria with the early breeze in our hair and watch the dawn come up over the sea. Or we would sit by the Nile and listen to the harps and timbrels as the great white moon went over above us. Timon. Timon, I want to say...I want to say...*(He gasps and clutches his chest.)* Timon! Red bottle! Quickly, quickly!

TIMON: Hang on! Hang on!

HEROD: The bottle, the bottle. And the green one!

TIMON: Are you all right? Is it working?

HEROD: Yes, yes, I believe it is. Timon, this is a special moment. Destiny is upon me.

TIMON: Eh?

HEROD: I must be fittingly arrayed. Bring me my robes, my royal robes. I must be ready.

TIMON: Oh, now wait. You're not going to the banquet?

HEROD: The robes, Timon. And the crown. I would have you bring me the crown.

TIMON: But – well, where is it?

HEROD: In my room, under the bed. You don't think I'd trust those fools at the treasury?

TIMON: Crown, right.

(TIMON begins to leave.)

HEROD: I would be worshipped in Egypt, you know. I may yet see my apotheosis.

TIMON: Apothewhat?

HEROD: Apotheosis. Come on, it's Greek. My ascension to divinity, to my place among the gods.

TIMON: Well, you always aimed high –

HEROD: Greek ones anyway. They're no better than me, most of them.

TIMON: I wonder if a bottle –

HEROD: I am above bottles. Bring the crown. And send for the High Priest.

TIMON: Again? What do you want the High Priest for? Oh.

HEROD: I need him most of all.

TIMON: But you're not – I mean, you can't be - . Oh, don't die. Please don't die.

(TIMON exits, distressed.)

HEROD: Ah, my fairest queen, thank you for being with me. It strengthens me. Not too far from Egypt, I trust? Not too wide the desert sands? But there never was any distance between us. Mariamne understood that: she knew she had married a man who could truly love two women. But she threatened me and I made a choice. The fault was hers, not mine. They told me you too were dead, but how could I believe it? Caesar, Anthony, they deserved their mortality, but you and I are above such little fates. Stand with me tonight, my queen, and I shall be a king forever.

TIMON: Here we are. I took the first thing in the wardrobe. Quite nice, I thought. I couldn't find the crown at first. You'd kicked it behind the po.

HEROD: Robe me, Timon. Make me ready.

TIMON: Right. Er, sire, if you don't mind me asking – ready for exactly what?

HEROD: You'll see.

TIMON: Oh, look! Here's the High Priest! Thank you for coming, sir –

HIGH PRIEST: What is it now? Not his bleating conscience again? Can't you drug him and give me peace?

TIMON: I'm sorry, really. I think – well – the way he's talking, this could be it.

HIGH PRIEST: What am I supposed to do? Fetch His sons.

TIMON: I don't think they'd help. I think he wants – er – spiritual solace. Or something. Oh, sir, do help him, please.

HIGH PRIEST: You do realise the entertainment's starting? Well, at least we'll have a sane king by the morning. Sire, I am here, to do your bidding. How may I serve you?

HEROD: I need you tonight. This is the hour of my destiny. My apotheosis.

HIGH PRIEST: Sire, Jews do not have apotheoses. We are permanently mortal.

HEROD: And I am not Jewish. I shall transcend everything.

HIGH PRIEST: My point is, sire, that if you wish to take your seat among the gods, I am not qualified to help you.

HEROD: You need do nothing. She will lead me, the divine queen. We will begin a marriage that will never end and I shall be a king eternally.

HIGH PRIEST: He's gone. Send for the guards, lock him up.

HEROD: My dynasty will extend through the ages. All you need do is crown me.

HIGH PRIEST: Crown you?

HEROD: Of course. Who but the High Priest should crown the king? The spiritual legitimises the temporal, you ought to know that.

HIGH PRIEST: You were crowned thirty years ago!

HEROD: This is different. You've got to do it tonight. You ought to be flattered, do you know that? I mean, the Proconsul of Asia's downstairs. I could have got him, but I chose you! And here you stand, in the presence of Cleopatra –

HIGH PRIEST: What?

HEROD: And all you have to do is put this thing on my head. Is that so much to ask?

HIGH PRIEST: Green bottle?

TIMON: There isn't a bottle for this. He'll come out of it.

HIGH PRIEST: When?

TIMON: Tomorrow, next month. I don't know.

HEROD: Will you stop muttering! Are you going to crown me or not?

HIGH PRIEST *(Stalling)*: If the senior priests were present –

TIMON: Just do it, sir, then get the guards.

HEROD: Never mind, I'll do it myself. What's the point of having you anyway? You're a shell, you're a hollow, walking shell. You cheated me! I longed for God and you gave me religion and philosophy. There's nothing inside you, there's nothing to give! Get out! Watch the dancing girls, murder children. Ahh, you're not so much an intellect as you like to appear. I feel the pride and hatred in your barren heart. Get away from me.

TIMON: He didn't mean it, sir –

HIGH PRIEST: Really? You understand that crumbling excuse for a mind? Time for a little Greek prayer. Good night.

(HIGH PRIEST exits.)

HEROD: It's time, my love, it's time.

TIMON: Greek prayer. I'd better.

HEROD: Ah, my Egyptian radiance, the cosmos awaits our rule.

TIMON: Right. Don't pray, just talk. Oh, God. Oh God, oh God, oh God, I've only done this once before, but listen to me and do something. Do that clarity thing again, that seemed to sort him out the last time. Just do it. Please.

HEROD: I need none of them. Priests and subjects, even emperors, what good are they? I am enough, sufficient unto myself. With my own hands, I take the crown of my universe –

(Timon bursts into tears.)

TIMON: Don't! Stop it, stop it!

(TIMON sobs. HEROD snaps out of it.)

HEROD: What's the matter with you?

TIMON: I don't want this! I don't want you to be mad, I don't want you to die! I can't stand it! What will I do when – when you - ? Who'll be father to me then?

HEROD: Father? Father: Timon's father. This is...real. A moment ago I was – somewhere in my mind. Don't tell me, I remember enough of it. Timon, I apologise. I heard you tell God himself you loved me, and I've been trying to outdo that with fantasies of power and a dead queen. I know it now: she only had eyes for Anthony, not me. I made it up, to comfort myself. But you're real, Timon. I forgot. Forgive me.

TIMON: Oh, nothing to forgive.

HEROD: I think there is. Let's have a little wine together and talk about it.

TIMON: Well, I'd like that. I'll see to it, shall I? I'm glad you're better. I like it when you're all right. If you're good, I'm good. I like just having you about, it makes me feel safe, sort of. *(Sings)* 'Light from your eyes shall shine in mine, beat of your heart within my breast.' We used to sing that at home. My mother liked it.

HEROD: Timon, help me lie down.

TIMON: Have you got a pain?

HEROD: No, no.

TIMON: Do you want a bottle? Red one?

HEROD: No more bottles, Timon. No bottles of any colour. Help me lie down.

TIMON: Now, never mind no more bottles. We've got to take our medicine, haven't we? Come over to the couch. There, is that better?

HEROD: Yes, yes. Thank you, Timon. I'm glad you're here.

TIMON: Well, faithful old hound, that's me.

HEROD: Come here. You know, the day they read my will, you'll discover you're no longer a servant and the owner of a villa and estate outside Athens.

TIMON: Oh, we're certainly having ideas tonight. Timon the landowner: that's rich.

HEROD: Timon, one of the reasons I even considered marrying Zibeah was that I thought there might be some little children who would love me as their father. And I would have loved them in return, if only for a few years. I have sons of course, but they're sons of my body, not of my heart. But I've not been without a son to love. Timon, you have been my son. Thank you. Thank you for ever.

TIMON: Sire? Are you asleep? Please be asleep. Oh no. No, no. I don't know what to do. I can't give you a bottle now. Tell me what to do, tell me - . Oh, wait, wait. I know what to do: I'll live my own life. You'd want that; any good father would. And I'll get a statue made, a little bronze statue of you, and I'll put it in the garden at Athens and say thank you to it every morning. And – and – here's your crown; I'll lay it on your chest. Put your hands round it. There. And there's a kiss for you. Well, I expect you'd like to be alone now. I'm glad you knew how I feel. Goodbye.

(A long pause, then HEROD wakes up.)

HEROD: I thought that was it. And so very easy. Dying appears to be no trouble at all: I'll finish it off in a moment. But not now, for you and I are alone together. I don't know your name, you're just the One Who listened to Timon. The clarity is with me again. I see things as they are and I want to say two things to you. Thank you for Timon's tears. That's a great gift. And the mercy. To my great surprise, I understand it, and I accept it. Very silly not to, considering the circumstances. I'm actually sorry: for Mariamne and everyone else. And the children, especially the children. I'm sorry, I'm sorry. Thank you – thank you for the mercy.

(He dies. As his hand falls, the crown is knocked to the floor and rolls away.)

The End.